My Grandparents Love Me

*With lots of love to Roger and Anne,
proud grandparents of Florence Grace* - **CF**

*Ai miei nonni, al nonno Garibaldi e alla nonna
che profumava di vaniglia, alla nonna nell'ombra
e al nonno elegante. Con tanto amore* - **JA**

SIMON AND SCHUSTER
First published in Great Britain in 2016 by Simon and Schuster UK Ltd
1st Floor, 222 Gray's Inn Road, London WC1X 8HB
A CBS Company

ISBN: 978-0-85707-585-7 (HB) • ISBN: 978-0-85707-586-4 (PB) • ISBN: 978-1-4711-4659-6 (eBook)
Printed in Italy • 10 9 8 7 6 5 4 3 2

My Grandparents Love Me

Claire Freedman & Judi Abbot

SIMON AND SCHUSTER

London New York Sydney Toronto New Delhi

I'm off to **Gran** and **Grandpa's**,
with a big smile on my face.

I always feel wrapped up in **love**,
when I stay at their place!

Gran's big welcome **hugs** are warm.

Wheeee!

Grandpa **swings** me round!

He laughs, "You're getting heavy," as my feet fly off the ground.

My room at Gran and Grandpa's house, has **special** toys there too.

Gran smiles, "Have you looked on your bed?

You might find
something **new!**"

Gran's baking is delicious, **yum!**
And when I munch and scoff
more cakes than Mum would let me eat,

Gran **never** tells me off!

Out at the funfair's **splish-splash** ride,

they don't mind getting **wet**.

POPCORN

Then off we go for ice creams, **slurp!**

The **biggest** we can get!

ROLL UP!

BALLOONS

ICE CREAM

I don't know how Gran's handbag,
which doesn't look **that** full,

has all we need
for our day out . . .

. . . it must be **magical!**

It's great to help in Grandpa's shed.
We build **amazing** things.

Gran hasn't seen our rocket —
ssshh!

It's red with silver wings.

Sometimes my Gran and Grandpa
will come to visit **me**.

We **all** go out together then,
it's so much **fun** —

yippeee!

Gran says I'll be a **champion** –
she's teaching me to swim.

With her beside me, I'm **not** scared.
Now I can **jump** right in!

Back home we all dress up and dance. Gran puts **loud** music on,

whilst funny Grandpa jokes about,
and does the steps all **wrong!**

"Let's read this story, Gran!" I say.
We **snuggle** in a chair.

Gran's silly voices make me laugh —
pretending she's the **bear!**

Warm from my bath and tucked in bed,
I yawn, "I've had such fun!"

"Us too," they smile
and kiss 'night-night'.

"We love you, little one!"